I0547200

NATHANIEL SHANNON
and the VANISHING TWIN

Trespasses

ALR011

Published by

Aqualamb

Nathaniel Shannon and the Vanishing Twin:
Nathaniel C. Shannon - vocals, guitars, bass, synths,
programming, saxophone, noise, complaining, guilt tripping
and rambling

Produced and recorded by Nathaniel C. Shannon
at various living crevices around New York City and Brooklyn, NY
2008-2016

"Lost Hills" engineered by Brandon Wiard at Pretty Suite Recording.
Ypsilanti, MI. Brandon Wiard played organ on "Lost Hills".
Adam Tatro played drums on "One Sixty Second Street"

All songs Written by Nathaniel C. Shannon

Mixed, mastered, and produced by Steve Austin
at Austin Enterprises 2016

All artwork and photography by Nathaniel C. Shannon
Vanishing Twin portrait photograph by Dean Chooch Landry
Book design by Eric Palmerlee

CONTENTS

The music for this release can be
downloaded via the link below:

http://aqualamb.org/011

DEBUTANTES

THE DEBUTANTES HAUNT
THE BOARDWALK.
THE SUN SETS IN
THEIR EYES.
THE SKY LOOKS DARK
AND CAUTIOUS.
IT'S TIME TO TAKE
THEIR LIVES.

AND I, I'M JUST
WAKING UP.

THEY SMELL SWEET
LIKE HONEY.
I CAN'T WAIT
TO GET THEM HOME.
THEIR SOFT WHITE SKIN'S
JUST LIKE PORCELAIN.
AND SLIPS RIGHT OFF
THE BONE.

AND I, I HAVE
A HUNGER TO FILL.
AND I, I WILL KEEP YOU
FOR MY MEAL.

THE TEETH AND FINGERS
WILL MAKE A NECKLACE.
THE LIPS I'LL PRESS
AGAINST MY OWN.
THE LEGS WILL
DO FOR BREAKFAST.
SHE WILL NEVER
AGAIN BE KNOWN.

AND I, I HAVE SO MUCH
TO SHARE.
AND I, I LOVE THAT
YOU ARE HERE.

ONE SIXTY SECOND STREET

THERE'S FIVE HEADS
SITTING ON AN ORGAN,
PAGES OF WORDS AND
DIAGRAMS TOO,
AN ALLIGATOR SNACKING
ON A COFFIN,
DARKNESS FALLS AND I
TAKE MY CUE.

THERE'S NO ROOMS LEFT
TO PAINT,
AND NO ROOMS LEFT
TO FILL,
THESE QUARTERS ARE
MUCH TOO SMALL,

TRAPPED IN THIS LIFE
WITH BOURBON AND A KNIFE,
BEHIND THESE PRISON WALLS.

THERE'S A WOLF DESCENDING
DOWN A MOUNTAIN,
THERE'S A WOLF FEASTING
UNDER THE MOON,
A MAN'S HEAD IS BLEEDING
AND THERE'S BLOOD ON
GIRLS HANDS,
THE DOCTOR SAID
A NEW FACE WILL DO

HOW WILL I BE SAVED?
IF THERE ARE ROACHES
IN MY GRAVE?
THERE DEER STARES ME
DOWN AND I DON'T MAKE
A SOUND,
AS I SLEEP ON THIS
VICTORIAN COUCH.

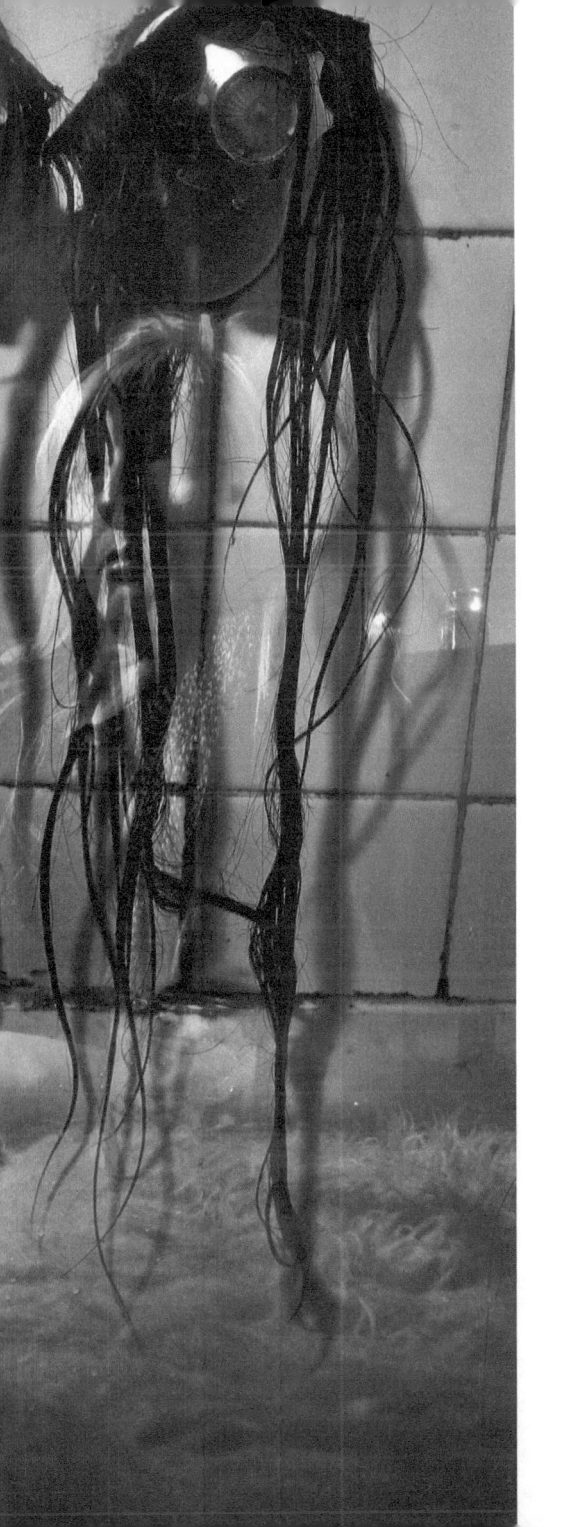

I SAW THAT WOLF DOWN BY THE RIVER
THE HOLY ONE WHO SPOKE IN TONGUES
TO HIS DAUGHTER
SHE ROSE SO HIGH THAT THE FEAR
IN HER EYES WAS GONE
AND THE RIVER TURNED TO ASH
AND THUNDER

THIS HAND BROKE THE SILENCE
OF OUR FATHERS
OUR FORTUNE IS TOLD BY OUR SINS
AND WHO ARE WE BUT THE DEVISE OF LIES
DESIGNED TO KEEP US MOVING FORWARD.

NO REGRETS ADVISED THE WARRIOR.

I SEE YOU STANDING NEXT TO HER GRAVE.
NO ONE WILL EVER KNOW
WHAT WE'RE THINKING
BLACK CLOUDS GIVE WARNING OF RAIN.
AND ONLY IN DREAMS WILL WE BE OK.

YOUR STARE GROWS DISTANT
LIKE THE HIGHWAY
YOUR EYES ARE SHARP, DARK AND IN PAIN.
I'D APOLOGIZE IF THE LIES
WEREN'T SO TRUTHFUL
BUT BABY MY SUIT FITS ANYWAY.

I KNOW THAT SHE CAN'T BE SAVED
I KNOW THAT THIS IS HER GRACE.
SO LET'S DO ANOTHER SHOT,
BECAUSE I HAVEN'T YET FORGOT
THAT THE DAY SHE DIES IS TODAY.

NO REGRETS ADVISED THE WARRIOR.

I SEE YOU STANDING NEXT TO HER GRAVE.
NO ONE WILL EVER KNOW
WHAT WE'RE THINKING
BLACK CLOUDS GIVE WARNING OF RAIN.
ONLY IN DREAMS WILL WE BE OK.

I SAW THAT WOLF DOWN BY THE RIVER
THE HOLY ONE WHO SPOKE IN TONGUES
TO HIS DAUGHTER
YOUR STARE GROWS DISTANT
LIKE THE HIGHWAY
NO ONE WILL EVER KNOW
WHAT WERE THINKING
I'D APOLOGIZE IF THE LIES
WEREN'T SO TRUTHFUL
THIS IS THE END FOR US ANYWAY.

AND THE RIVER TURNED TO ASH
AND THUNDER

BASTARD BLOOD

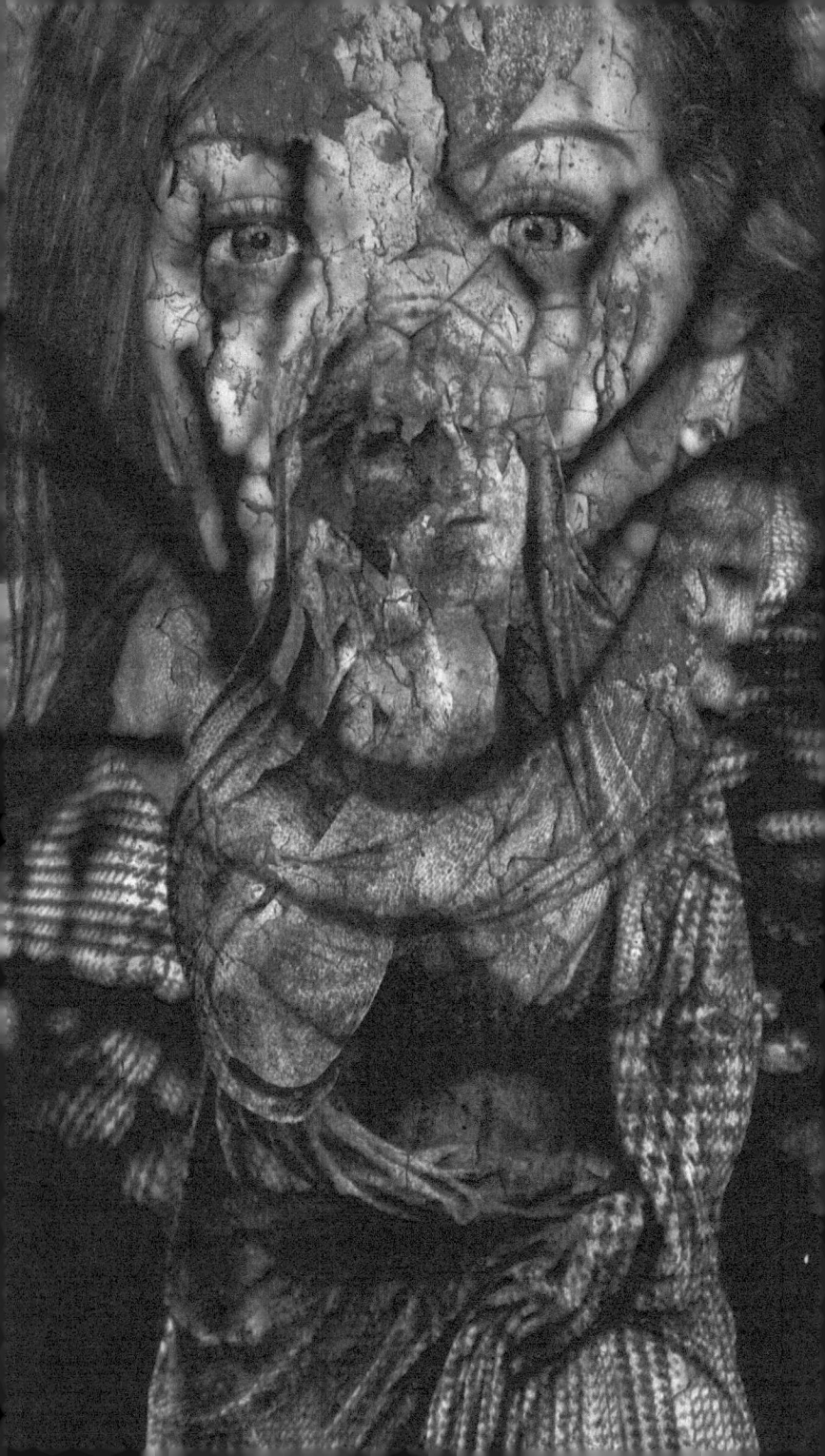

YOUR BLACK HAIR FALLS
IN YOUR FACE
I'D BRUSH IT ASIDE BUT I MIGHT DIE
ANOTHER TIME AND PLACE
BASTARD BLOOD STILL CRUISES
THROUGH MY VEIN

AND YOU, YOU ARE CURSED
WITH A BROKEN HEART
BUT AM I THE WORST?
I WOULD APOLOGIZE IF I COULD
BUT THE NIGHT STILLS LIES
AND WE BOTH KNOW
I'M NO GOOD.

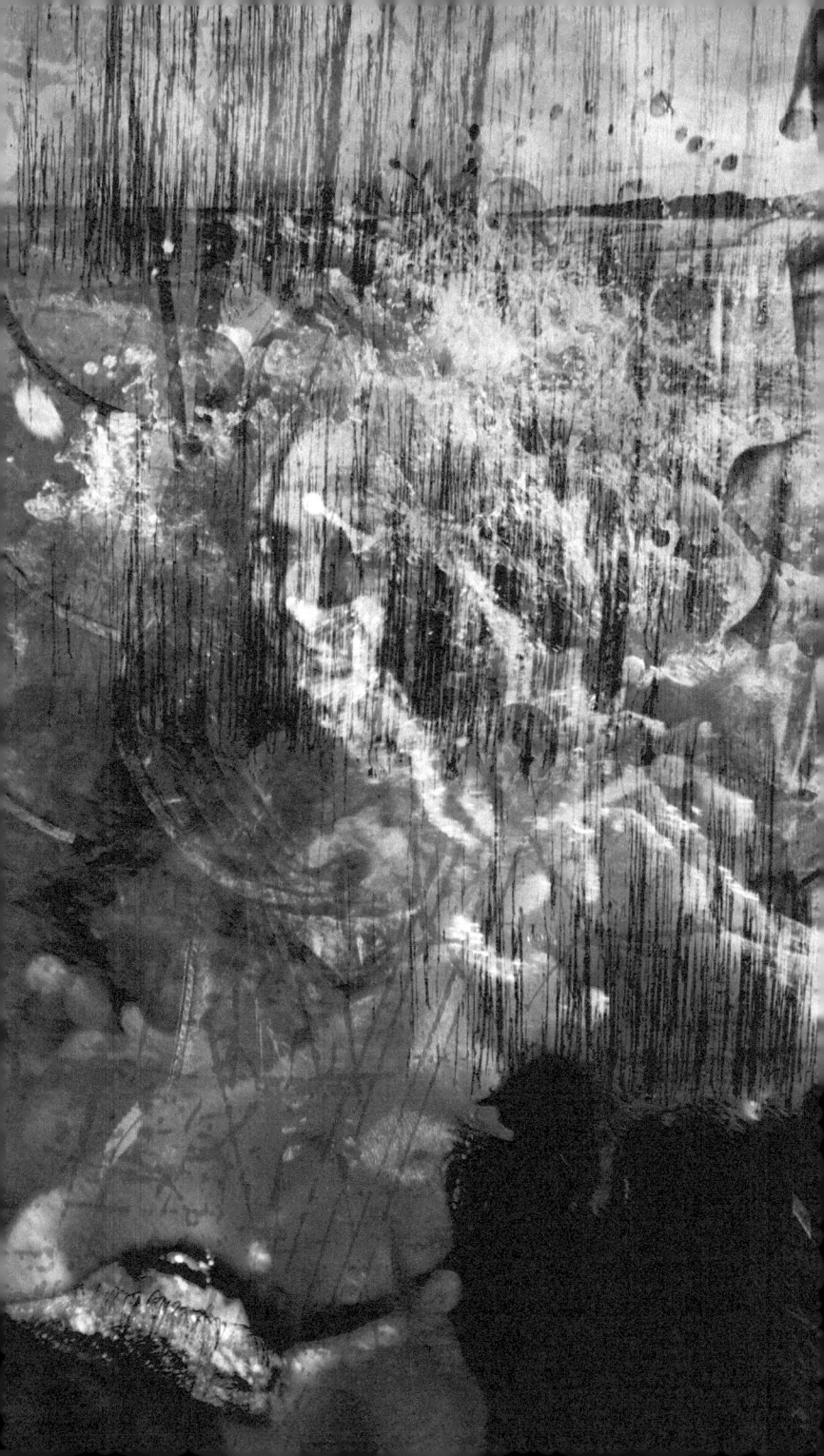

THIS IS THE HARDEST YEAR
LIKE A CHILD I AM FILLED
 WITH FEAR
WE DO THE BEST WE CAN
BUT THE NIGHT STILL LIES
AND IT'S HARD TO UNDERSTAND

YOUR BLACK HAIR FALLS
 IN YOUR FACE
I'LL BRUSH IT ASIDE FOR
ANOTHER NIGHT
PUT IT BACK IN IT'S PLACE
A DIFFERENT HEART
BUT THE SAME FACE

AND YOU, YOU'VE CHANGED
AS WELL SOME TIME APART
 AND A LITTLE HELL.
WE TAKE IT BACK IF WE COULD
BUT THE NIGHT IS NEW AND
WE BOTH ARE MISUNDERSTOOD

 AND THREE YEARS LEADS TO
NEW FEARS THAT SCARES US
 TO THE BONE
AND THREE YEARS LEADS
TO NEW FEARS WITH TIME
 TO BE ALONE
AND THREE YEARS BRINGS
US BACK
 AND YOUR BLACK HAIR FALLS

CONVERSATIONS OF BLOODLUST AND MORALITY

I SEE YOU THROUGH
SMOKE AND COCAINE.
THE THUNDER'S ALL
I HEAR. FLASH BULBS
ILLUMINATE YOUR
FACE. CHEERS TO
YOU NEAR ME IN
TEARS.

I TELL YOU THAT
I'M SORRY. I TELL
YOU THAT I CARE.

I'LL BRING YOU BACK
TO MY HOUSE LET
ME SAVE YOU
FROM YOUR HOME.
HELP YOU OUT OF
YOUR WE CLOTHES.
I HATE TO SLEEP
ALONE.

YOU TELL ME THAT
YOU'RE SORRY. YOU
TELL ME THAT YOU
CARE.
  YOU'RE LIPS SO SOFT
AND HAIR SO SWEET.
  DO YOU EVEN KNOW
WHERE YOU ARE?
  I CARVE MY NAME
ACROSS YOUR SKIN.
  FROM THIGH TO
MOUTH.

YOU TELL ME THAT
YOU'RE SORRY.
YOU TELL ME THAT
YOU'RE SCARED.
I TELL YOU I'M NOT
SORRY. I TELL YOU
I DON'T CARE...
AT ALL.

YOUR SKIN CUTS
WITH SUCH EASE.
I HAVEN'T EATEN
LIKE THIS IN YEARS.
MY TONGUE SOAKS
UP YOUR BLOOD.
DRINK YOU
FROM EAR TO EAR.

I HEARD YOU SAY I'M
SORRY. I HEARD YOU
SAY YOU'RE SCARED.
I LIED WHEN I SAID
I CARE, AT ALL.

LOST
HILLS

I SEE YOUR SHADOW AGAINST THE WALL.
 WALKING TOWARDS TO THE DOOR.
I'M TOO MUCH TO HANDLE OR BE IGNORED.

   I'M WALKING DOWN LOST HILLS,
    LOOKING FOR WHERE WE LEFT OFF.
   THE BANDAGES TO HEAL US,
    CAN'T HEAL ENOUGH.

   TONIGHT WE BLEED AS ONE.
    FAST ASLEEP ALONE IN TIME.
   WITH YOUR SOFT SKIN AND KILLING EYES.
    KILL TO MAKE YOU MINE.

AND WHAT ABOUT THAT CARD?
DRAWN WITH INK TO MAKE ME THINK.
 YOU CARED, PACKED AWAY IN A BOX
SOMEWHERE.

   YOU'RE SO, HOLLYWOOD, BABY.
    YOU'RE SO, LIKE HEROIN, HONEY.
   YOU'RE SO, HOLLYWOOD, BABY.
    YOU'RE SO, DANGEROUS, DARLING.

 THERE WAS THIS DREAM I HAD.
 WE WERE YOUNG AND YOU WERE THERE,
  DRIVING DOWN ROUTE ONE WITH
  A PURPLE ORCHID IN YOUR HAIR.

   WE STOPPED ALONG THE BEACH.
    DUG OUR FEET INTO THE SAND.
   I TOLD YOU ALL MY TROUBLES
    AND YOU HELD MY HAND.

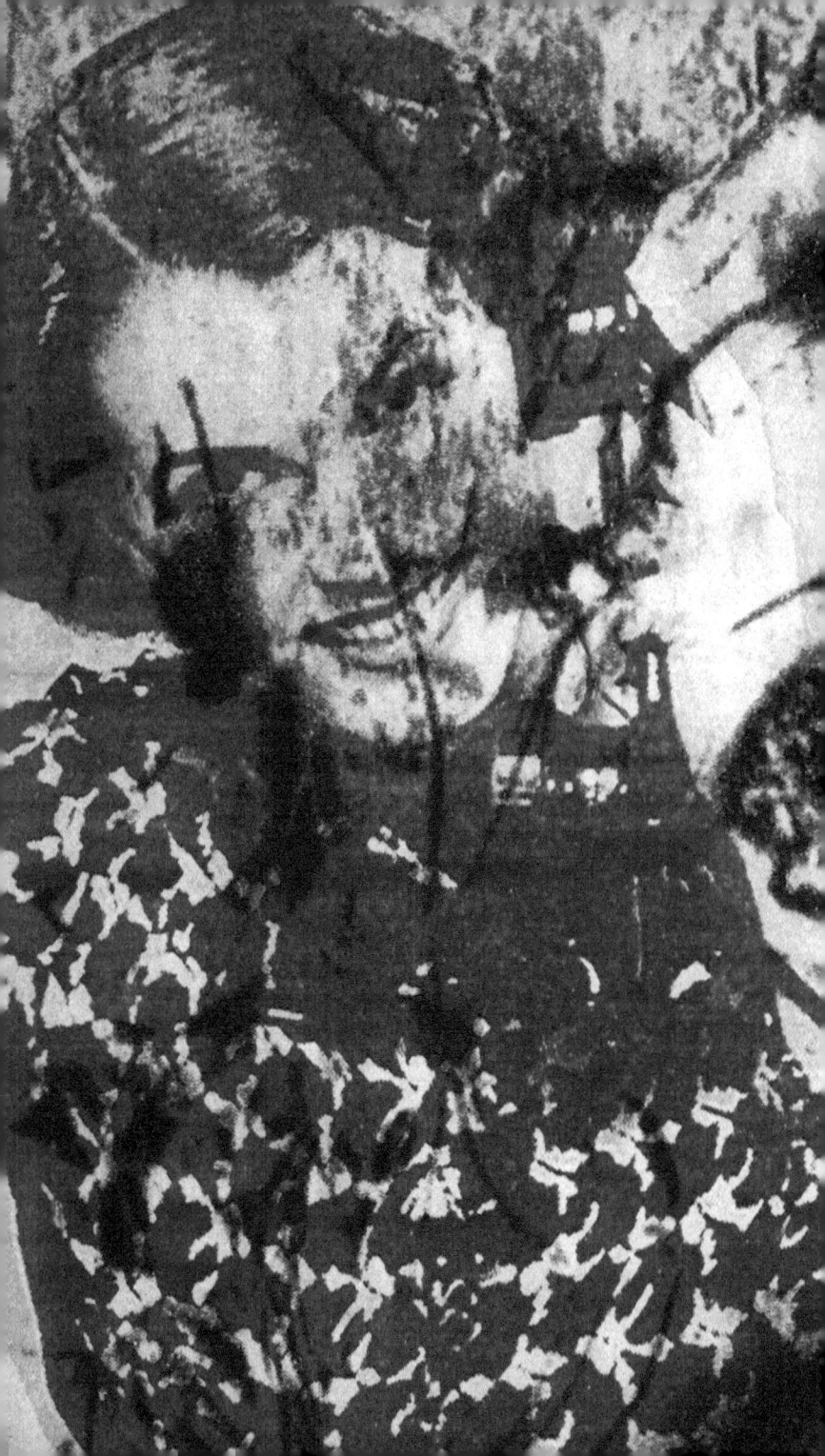

DECEPTION PROJECTION

TODAY IS THE DAY I SAY I'M GOING TO CHANGE.

CONTENT OF
ATTRACTION

PUT THE BABY IN THE BAGGY,
PACK IN FLOWERS BLOOD AND
 TIME, A LOCAL ACCOUNT
OF ROMANCE, THE PERFECT
VALENTINE'S CRIME.

A SURPRISE VISITATION
 WITH A STAB WOUND
TO BLEED, THE CONTENT
 OF ATTRACTION TO ME.

CHOKE ON MY FINGERS,
 THERE'S NO RING SO IT
LINGERS, COMMITMENT
TO NOTHING, MAKES US
 FREE UP FOR SOMETHING.

CLEAN UP FOR A NEW
LOVER, WASH YOUR HANDS
OF EACH OTHER,
 AND WAIT TO DIG
ONE ANOTHER A GRAVE.

BURN YOURSELF ALIVE,
JUST TO FEEL FINE,
JUST A LITTLE
ATTENTION, KEEP
TOUCHING YOURSELF,
YOU'VE COMMITTED
NO CRIMES. DUST OFF
THE MOTEL SHEETS,
AT MIDNIGHT WE ARE
WEAK, DON'T LOCK US
OUT OF THE ROOM, IN
EACH OTHERS TORTURE
WE ARE CONSUMED.

SLAP ACROSS THE
FACE, BLOOD FALLS
TO THE FLOOR, LICK
UP THE DROPLETS,
FOR YOU THERE'S
ALWAYS MORE.

CLEAN UP FOR A NEW
LOVER, WASH YOU
HANDS OF EACH OTHER,
AND WAIT TO DIG ONE
ANOTHER A GRAVE.

HALO

WHAT'S UNDER THE HALO,
  THAT CAUSES SUCH A SCENE?
DO MAN, WOMAN OR CHILD,
REALLY KNOW WHAT IT MEANS.

FEAR CAN LEAD TO BLINDNESS,
AND BLINDNESS LEADS TO FEAR,
JUST BECAUSE YOU CAN'T SEE A MAN,
  DOES THAT MEAN HE'S NOT HERE?

WHAT'S UNDER THE HALO,
  THAT GUILTS US CONSTANTLY,
OUR BIG BRIGHT EYES,
OUR GOLDEN HAIR,
WE PRAY,
WE SING,
WE SEEM...

TO FIND OUR WAY BACK ON DOWN,
WHERE HABITS DON'T FAR OFF ROAM,
  UNDERNEATH THE HALO,
WERE LOOKING FOR OUR HOME.

TOMBS

AN UNJUST ARREST FOR A TOOL OF SELF DEFENSE, SECOND AMENDMENTS DON'T MEAN ANYTHING ANYMORE, WITH PARANOID COPS, ARRESTING THE WHOLE BLOCK, WHERE HAS OUR NEIGHBORHOOD GONE?

GRAVITY CAN PULL DOWN ANYTHING.
GRAVITY HAS IT'S HOLD ON ME.

THE SEAFOAM GREEN WALLS OF THE TOMB,
ARE THE SAME COLOR, AS MY CHILDHOOD HOME,
STEEL BARS HOLD US IN, WITH NO WHERE TO
ROAM, THE SMELL OF SHIT, IS MAKING ME SICK.

HOW LONG WILL I BE HERE? HOW LONG
MUST I WAIT? THE PRICE TO PAY
FOR PROTECTION, COST MORE BONES

THAN I MAKE.
BECAUSE OF THE GUILT OF ASSOCIATION,
I WISH TO NOT KNOW MYSELF,
I'VE LEARNED MORE INSIDE HERE,
THAN INSTITUTIONS THINK IS GOOD

FOR MY HEALTH

MY BABY'S AT HOME, CRYING TEARS BY THE
PHONE, SHE'S PATIENTLY WAITING TO HEAR
MY VOICE, SAY IT'S ALRIGHT, BUT THERE'S
NO END IN SIGHT, THE BREAD IS HARD AND

MY STOMACH, IS FULL OF HELL,
TO BRIDE AND GROOM I WISH YOU WELL,
THE PRICE TO PAY FOR PROTECTION,
COST MORE BONES THAN I MAKE.

TRESPASSES

TONIGHT WE WRITE LIES AND SMILE AT THE TIME,
WHILE MY EYES DRY OUT, SHADOWS MORE
AROUND MY HEAD.

DESPITE MY WORDS, AND WHAT YOU'VE HEARD,
THERE IS REALLY NOTHING TO SAY. THE FOOL,
THE BASTARD, YEAH ALL OF US, PRAY TO
STAY AWAY.

I'M ON A ROLL WHEN YOU STEAL MY SOUL,
I CAN NOT SWALLOW THE TRUTH ANY
BETTER THAN YOU.

SO TAKE MY EVIDENCE OFF THE WALL,
AND TELL ME WHERE I WENT WRONG.

SACRIFICE MY WORDS.
JUST TO HAVE THAT FEELING AGAIN.
AFTER THE WINTERS GONE,
LETS NOT PRETEND,
AND DO IT ALL OVER AGAIN.

OH LORD. LEAVE ME HERE.
OH LORD. MEET ME HERE.

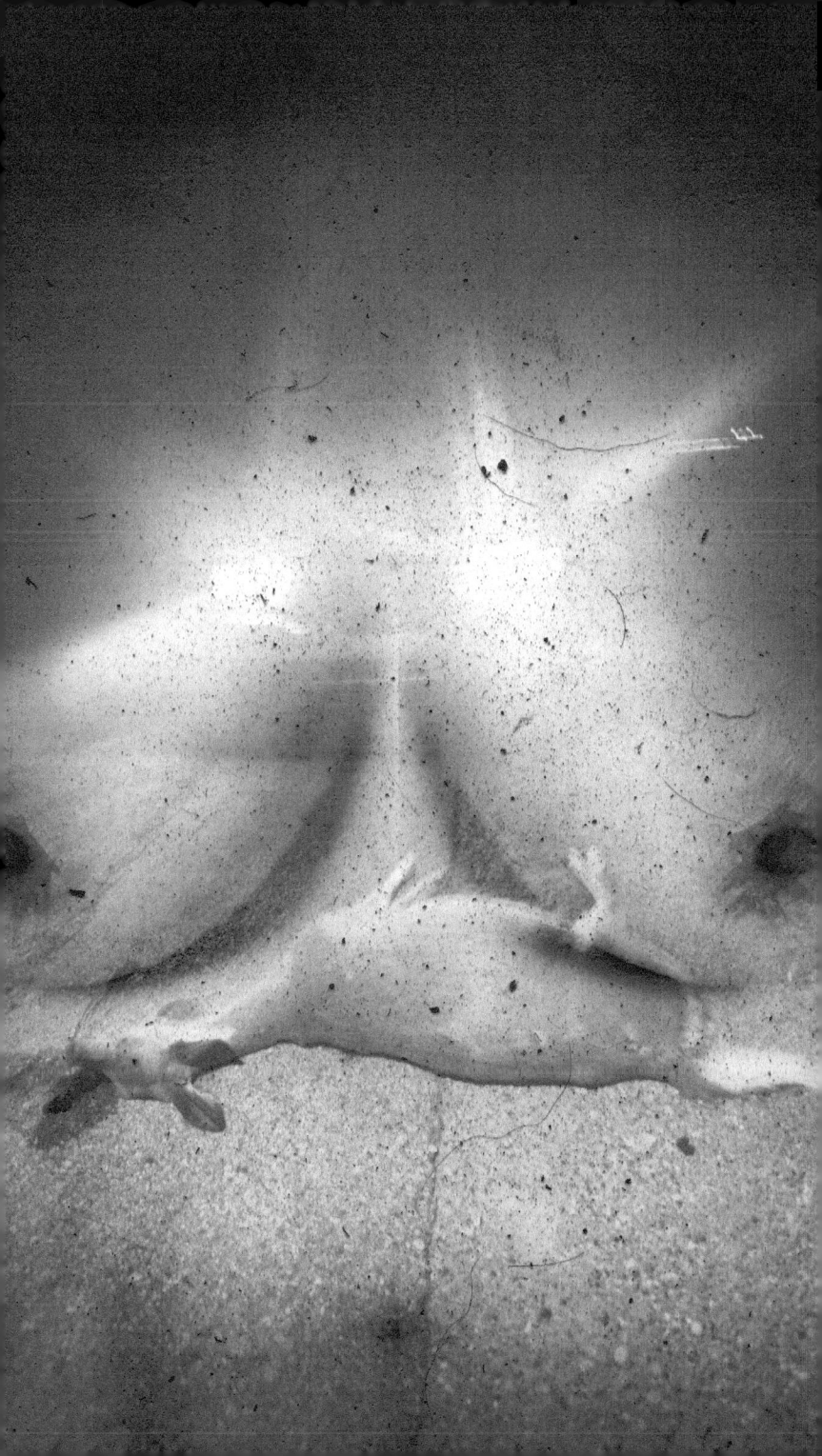

OPEN LETTER
TO THE CITY
OF ANN ARBOR

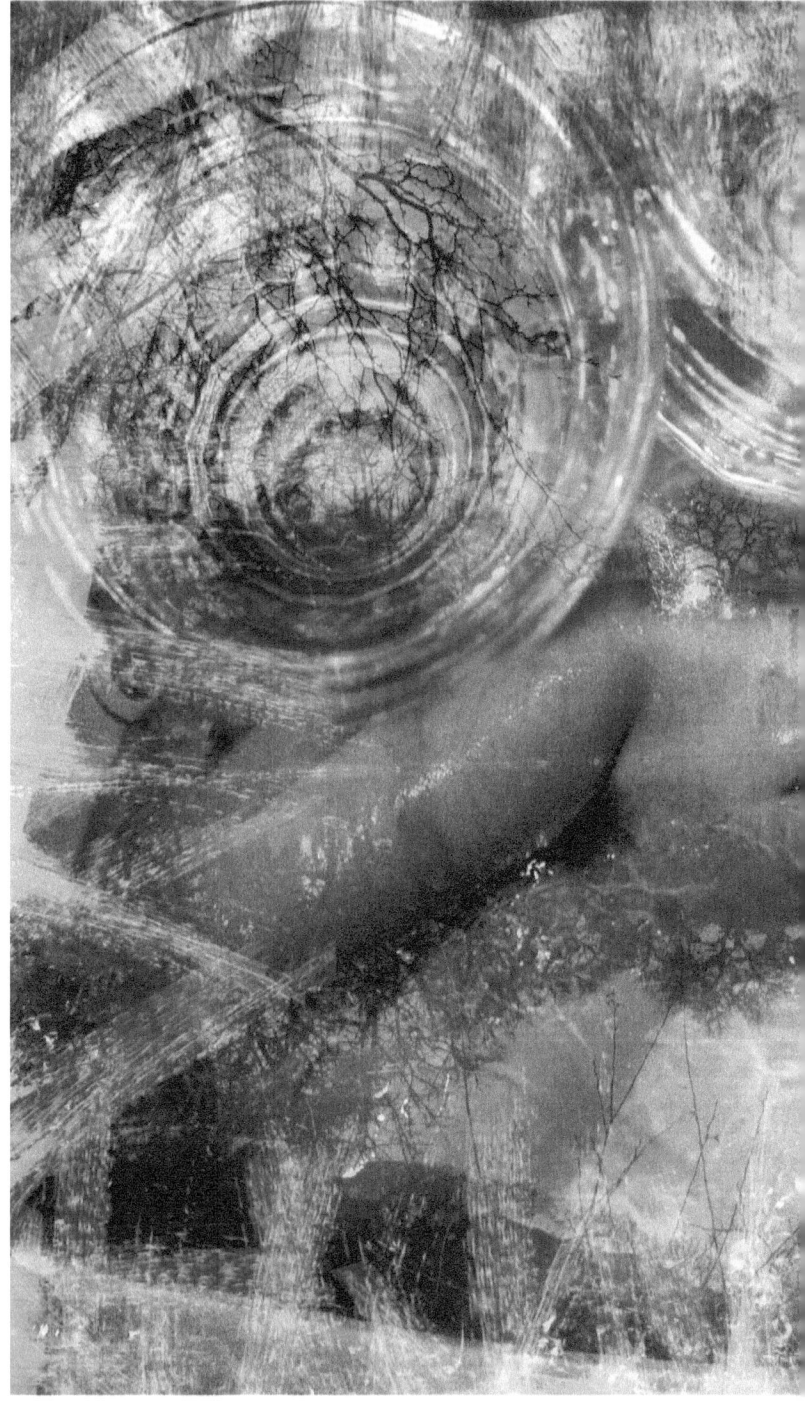

JUST BECAUSE I'M A BASTARD
DOESN'T MEAN, I'LL LEARN ANY FASTER
 SO I LIE AWAKE WHILE THE EARTH
SLEEPS THE MOON
AND I LIE AWAKE WHILE I SLEEP NEXT
TO YOU.

  MY BOTTLE,
  IS ALMOST EMPTY
   ANOTHER ROUND,
  AND WE'LL SEE WHAT
  YOU MEAN TO ME
  WE LIE AWAKE WHILE
  YOU HAVEN'T GOT A CLUE
  WE LIE AWAKE WHILE
  I THINK ABOUT YOU.

TAKE CARE, I'M SO CONTAGIOUS
 YOUR DIARY, HAS RIPPED OUT PAGES
WRAPPED UP, IN BLANKETS AND BULLSHIT
I DON'T KNOW HOW TO BE ANYONE ELSE.

SO QUIET, MY WORDS SPILL LIKE WHISKEY
PLEASE DON'T GO, IT'S A LONG WAY BACK
 TO YPSI
WHO'S TURN IS IT TO STAB ANOTHER BACK
WHO'S TURN IS IT TO FILL IN THE CRACKS.

  SWIMMING AT NIGHT,
   WHILE YOU WERE FAST ASLEEP.
  NAKED, UNDER THE MOON LIGHT.
    MAKING, MORE SECRETS WE HAD TO KEEP.

AND BY MORNING THE WHOLE TOWN KNEW.
 AND LIKE ALWAYS, EVERYONE BUT YOU.

NOW YOU KNOW, I'M A BASTARD
YOUR INCESTRAL HEART BEATS FASTER
SO I LIE AWAKE WHILE THE EARTH SLEEPS
 THE MOON
AND I LIE AWAY WHILE I DRINK AWAY YOU.

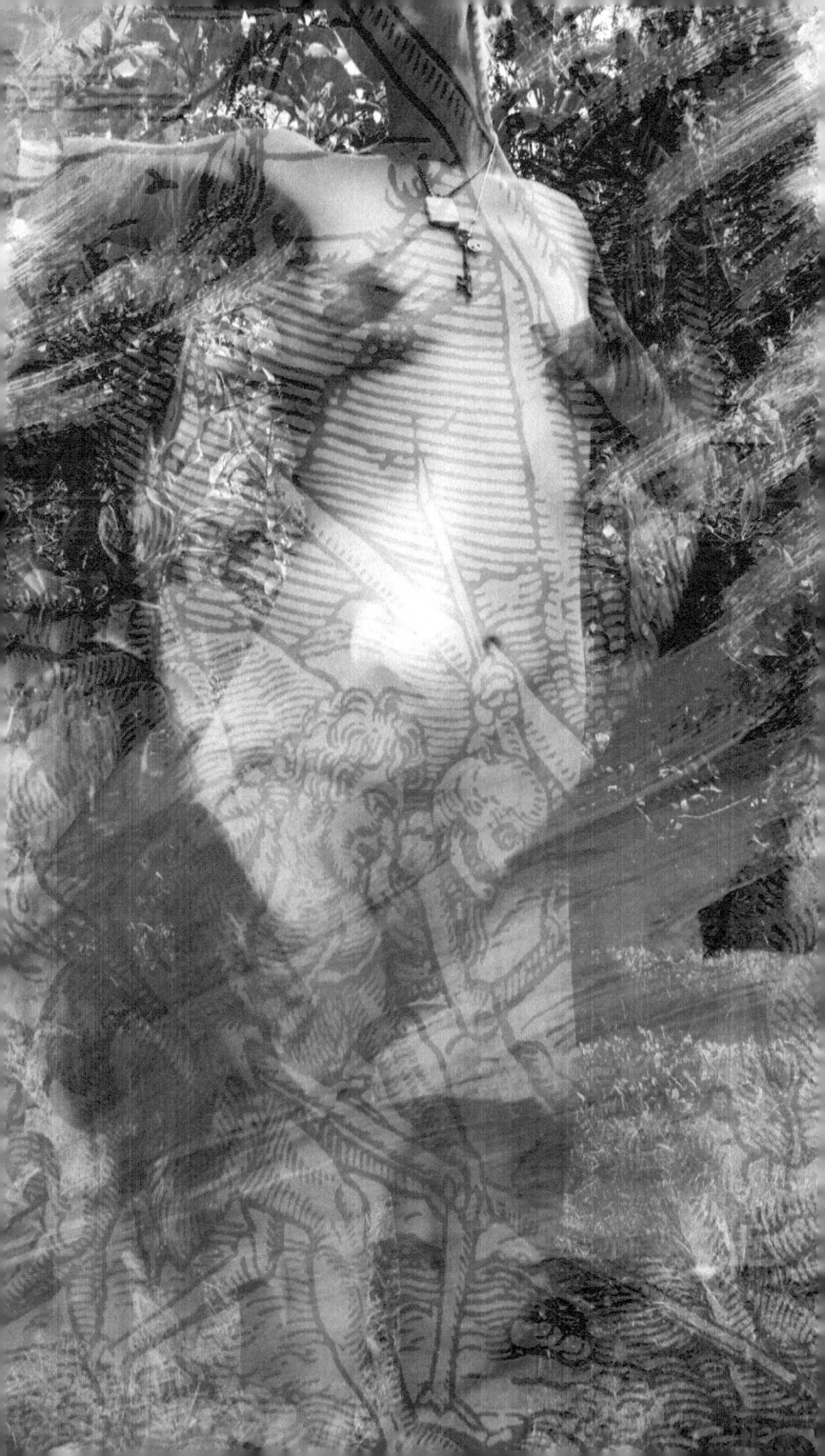

COLMA

WE LIVE IN A CITY
BUILT ON THE
BONES OF OTHERS
AND ISN'T IT
PRETTY BABY
THE WAY THAT
WE SURVIVE

I ASKED A MAN
ABOUT THE
SILENCE

I BARELY HEARD
WHAT HE SAID

BUT HE SPOKE
OF THE LIVING
BEING OUT

NUMBERED BY

THE DEAD

ONLY A FEW HOURS
UNTIL IT'S LIGHT
AND THE DEAD

RETURN TO
THE GROUND

WE WORK IN A CITY
TENDING TO THE
GRAVES OF THE
DEAD

TIME
AS COFFIN

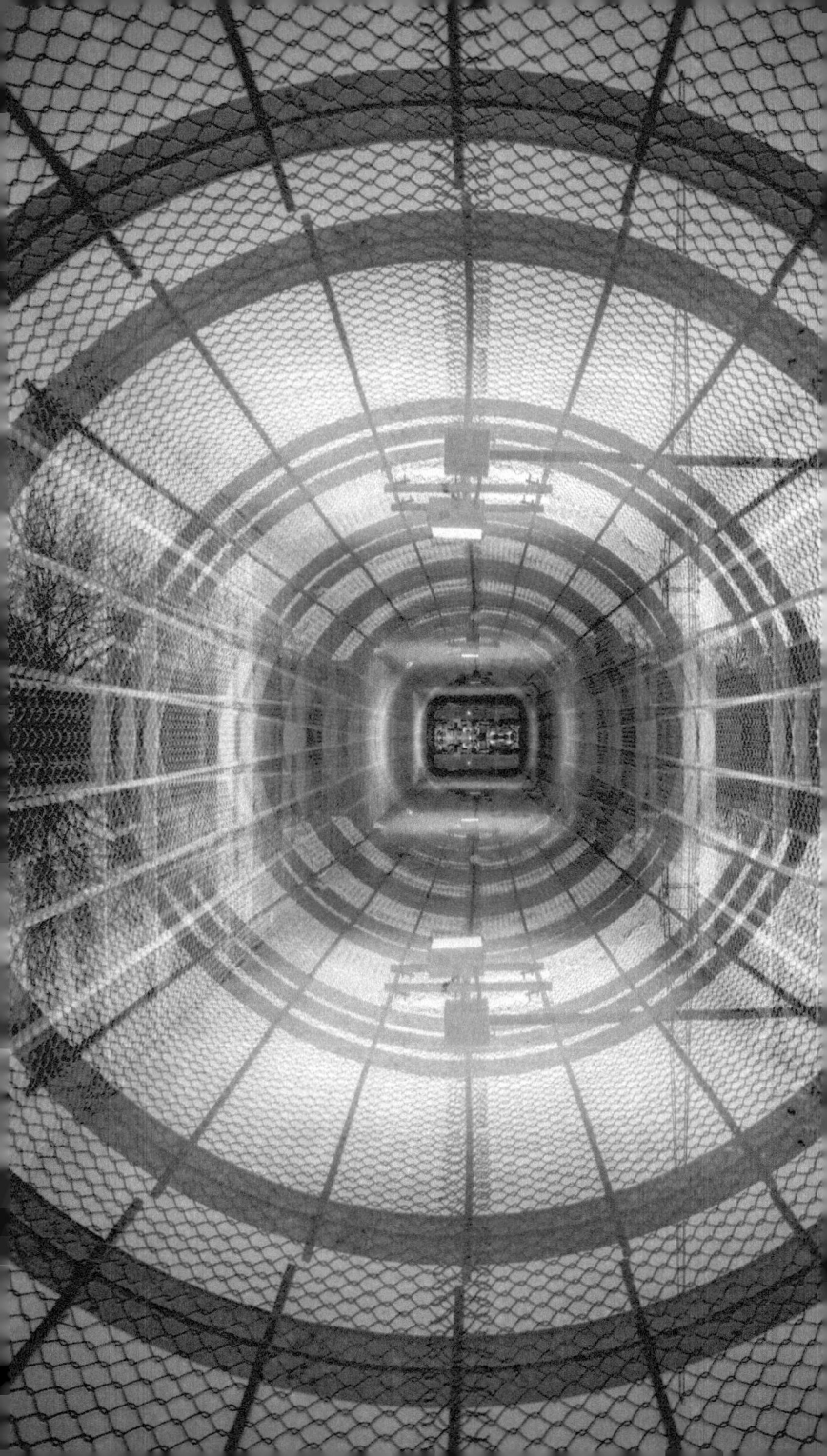

YOU MAKE THE WORLD BY WHISPERS.
YOU MAKE THE WORLD YOU SEE.
THE WORLD HERE IS MY BONE CAVE.
I SHALL NOT WANT, I SHALL NOT LEAVE.

IT'S ALL JUST PISS AND WINE.
WE'RE DOING JUST FINE.

YOU SAY TIME AS COFFIN.
I SAY I HAVE HANDS IN THE DUST.
THE PAGES OF THE BIBLE ARE BURNING.
SO LETS MAKE ANOTHER ONE UP.

THIS DRAIN IS CLOGGED WITH HOLY WATER.
THIS PEW IS MUCH TOO SMALL.
I THINK THIS TANK NEEDS LIQUOR.
I THINK THIS MAN NEEDS SCRIPTURE.

HEAVENLY CREATURE.
GET ON WITH YOUR CONFESSION.
THE WORDS THAT YOU LIVE BY.
SEEM TO BE IN QUESTION.

SO PICK UP YOUR STICK.
AND TEACH US ALL YOU KNOW.
WHERE WE LAY OUR HEADS DOWN.
IS THE PLACE WE CALL HOME.

NEVER DRINK
DEAD BLOOD

A WORKING MAN'S JOB,
A CHILD AND A WIFE,
ALL THAT WAS TO DESIRE,
UNTIL THEY LOST THEIR LIVES.

I WALKED THE EDGE OF NIGHT,
LOOKING FOR RUM, WHORES AND DEATH,
UNTIL A STRANGER APPROACHED ME,
AND I TOOK MY LAST BREATH.

I WAS GIVEN A CHOICE,
WHETHER TO LIVE OR TO SURVIVE,
TO SEE THE BEAUTY OF THE WORLD,
BUT ONLY IF BY NIGHT.

I HEARD HIS WORDS,
AND SMELLED THE AIR,
AND HANDED OVER MY LIFE,
ERASING THE MEMORIES OF
A HOME, A CHILD, A WIFE.
A HOME, A CHILD, A WIFE.

HE EXPLAINED TO ME,
ALL I NEEDED TO KNOW,
SET THE PAST ABLAZE,

AND FOLLOWED HIM HOME,
ALWAYS REMEMBER HE SPOKE WITH MUCH LOVE,
NEVER, NO NO NEVER DRINK DEAD BLOOD.

FOR CENTURIES I DANCED AND DRAINED
  THE WORLD AROUND,
UNTIL DEATH DID CHANGE IN A WOMAN
  I HAD FOUND,
HER INNOCENCE I DID SPARE, HER BLOOD
  BELONGED TO US,
MY LOVER SHE BECAME WITH
  THE SAME BLOODLUST.

I EXPLAINED TO HER,
ALL SHE NEEDED TO KNOW,

  SET THE PAST ABLAZE,
WE MADE OUR NEW HOME,
ALWAYS REMEMBER I SPOKE

  WITH MUCH LOVE,
NEVER, NO NO NEVER
DRINK DEAD BLOOD.

HER THIRST WAS GREAT AND HER
CONSCIOUS WAS NUMB,
I WAS BEGINNING TO WORRY WHAT
SHE HAD BECOME,
A PREDATOR FOR SPORT,
RATHER FOR OUR NEED,
SHE ENJOYED JUST WATCHING,
MEN AND WOMEN BLEED.

SHE LAUGHED AND PLAYED AND BATHED
IN THEIR BLOOD,
QUICKLY I REALIZED IT WAS NO LONGER
ME SHE LOVED,
WITH ALL THE PAIN IT CAUSED MY
BLACK HEART,
MY LOVER AND HER LUST HAD
TO BE STOPPED.

SO I GRABBED HER BY HER HAIR AND BOUND
 HER BY HER WRISTS,
THE SCENT OF HER BODY AND SKIN
 I WOULD MISS,
I CHAINED HER TO A TREE AND WAITED
 FOR THE SUN TO RISE,
SHE CURSED AT ME AND SPIT ON ME
 WAILING HER CRIES,
A VICTIM LONG SENSE DEAD I DRAINED
 FROM THE NECK,
DRINKING FROM HER FLESH I KNEW WHAT
 WOULD COME NEXT,
MY LOVER WOULD BE DESTROYED
 IN THE FRESH MORNING SUN,
AND WITH THAT I WOULD PERISH
 FROM DRINKING DEAD BLOOD.

NEVER EVER NEVER DRINK DEAD BLOOD.
IT MIGHT JUST POISON BOTH OF US.

THANKS IN NO PARTICULAR ORDER:

Peggy and R. Timothy Shannon
Jason Fahlstrom
Eric and Johnathan at Aqualamb
Dave and Allison Graw
Brian and Marie Haller
Rachael Salerno
Michael Aul
Bret Wisniewski
Angelo Pournaras
John Fisher
Toby Trier
Kendra Morris
Lisa Guariglia
Meridith Nicholaev
Jess Phelps
Kevin Day
Chris Bathgate
Anthony Gentile
Devin Yalkin
Brandon Wiard
Elisa Marie Soto
Sean Gresens
Adam Tatro
Howard Chang
Thomas Beddow
Claire Skowronek
Nicholas Maglione
Jessica Somerhausen
Amy Campbell
Vincent Castiglia
Brooke Travis
Jeff Tuttle

Derek Swanson
Damien and Francesca Moyal
Paul Parkanzky
Jeff Gensterblum
Dan Janquint
Michael Gaffey
Sean Hoen
Josch Chodakowsky
Joseph Collins
Joseph Violet
Thom Kikot / 89X
Craig Gaulzetti
Jesse James Madre
Dean Chooch Landry
Tucker Rule
Steve Karp And Yuppicide
Heads Will Roll
Child Bite
Descender
Small Brown Bike
Starflyer59
Goatwhore
Tiger Flowers
Thursday
Bwhc

Arty, George, and St. Vitus Crew

And Mr. Steve Austin and Today Is The Day, for all the help working on this record, your friendship and endless mentoring

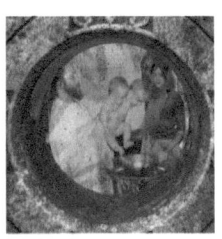

The music for this release can be
downloaded via the link below:

http://aqualamb.org/011